This Little Tiger book
belongs to:

_____   _____

_____   _____

_____   _____

For Tilda Oya.
Special thanks to
Lisa Taniyama for her help,
and to Maudie, Ella and Jude
for making this book possible
– Lomp

LITTLE TIGER PRESS LTD,
an imprint of the Little Tiger Group
1 Coda Studios,
189 Munster Road,
London SW6 6AW
www.littletiger.co.uk

First published in Great Britain 2019
This edition published 2020
Text and illustrations copyright © Lomp 2019
Lomp has asserted his right to be identified as
the author and illustrator of this work under
the Copyright, Designs and Patents Act, 1988
A CIP catalogue record for this book is
available from the British Library

Printed in China
LTP/1400/3075/0120
10 9 8 7 6 5 4 3 2 1

Adventurers'
Flea Market

WILFRED AND OLBERT's
EPIC PREHISTORIC ADVENTURE

Written and illustrated by *Lomp*

LITTLE TIGER
LONDON

Quick as a flash, Ollie pulls Will into the time portal!

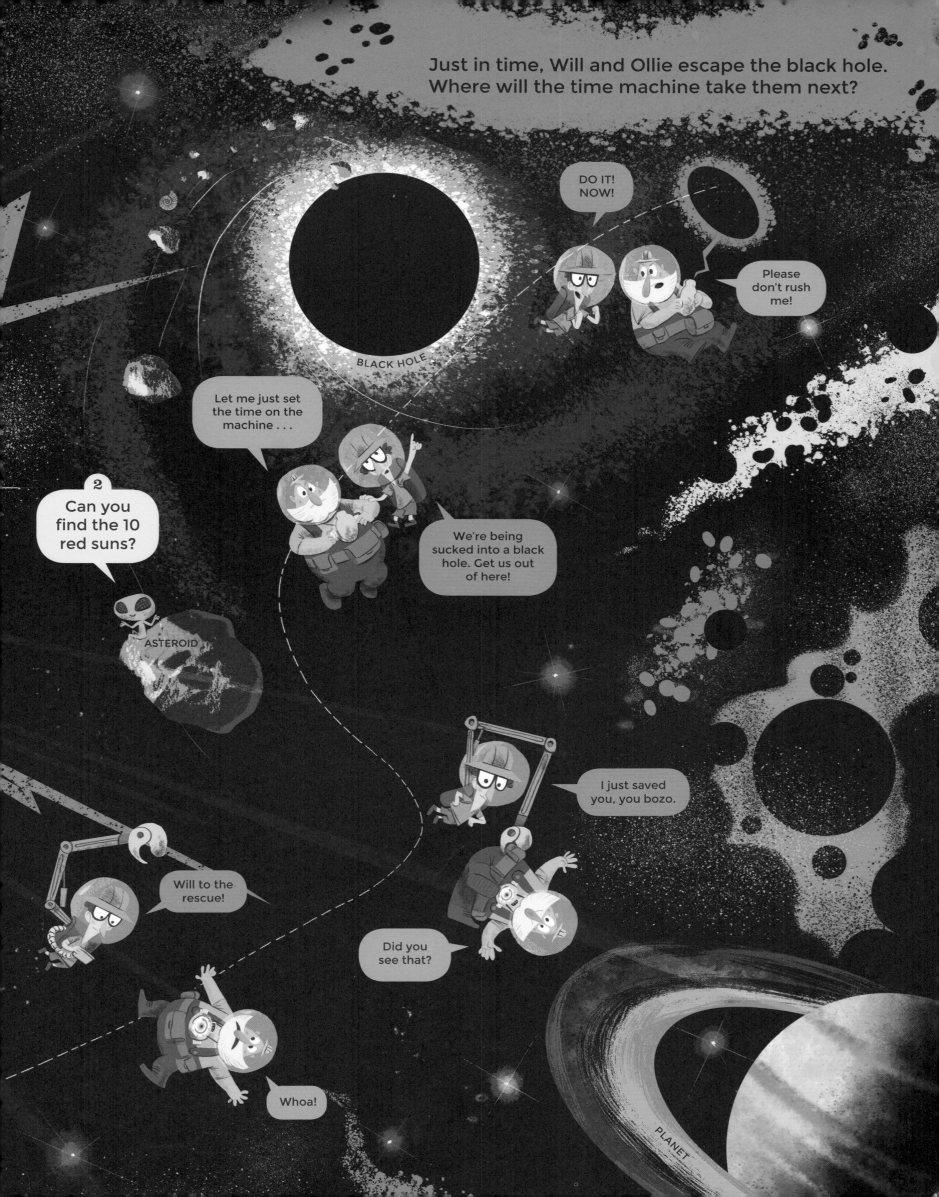

Wilfred and Olbert dive into the portal.
Will they get back home?

The monkey has run off with the time machine.
OH NO! Will Ollie and Will be lost in time for ever?

BRRRR! Will and Ollie follow the monkey through the portal into an ice age in the Quaternary period. Will they get their time machine back?

. . . arrive back home, just in time for tea! HOORAY!

At last, Wilfred and Olbert can relax.

Here are the solutions to the puzzles. Did you solve them all?

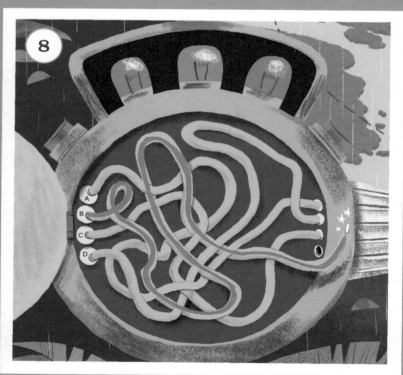

Psst! I'm hidden throughout the book in 11 different places! Can you find all of them?

Want to learn how to pronounce "Coelophysis" and "Ankylosaurus"?
Visit: www.littletiger.co.uk/tiger-blog/dinosaur-pronounciation

More epic adventures from Little Tiger . . .